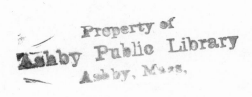
An amusing Turkish silly tale, in which a foolish old couple, with the kindest of intentions, go to visit their married daughter and cause her no end of problems in their efforts to be of help.

HILILI AND DILILI

BARBARA K. WALKER

A TURKISH SILLY TALE

ADAPTED FROM A TURKISH FOLK TALE TRANSLATED
BY MRS. NERIMAN HIZIR IN ANKARA, TURKEY

ILLUSTRATED BY BILL BARSS

FOLLETT PUBLISHING COMPANY
CHICAGO

To Neriman Hizir, *Ayse Abla,*
beloved of all Turkish children
and young people

Library of Congress Catalog Card Number: 65-13270

123456789

HILILI AND DILILI

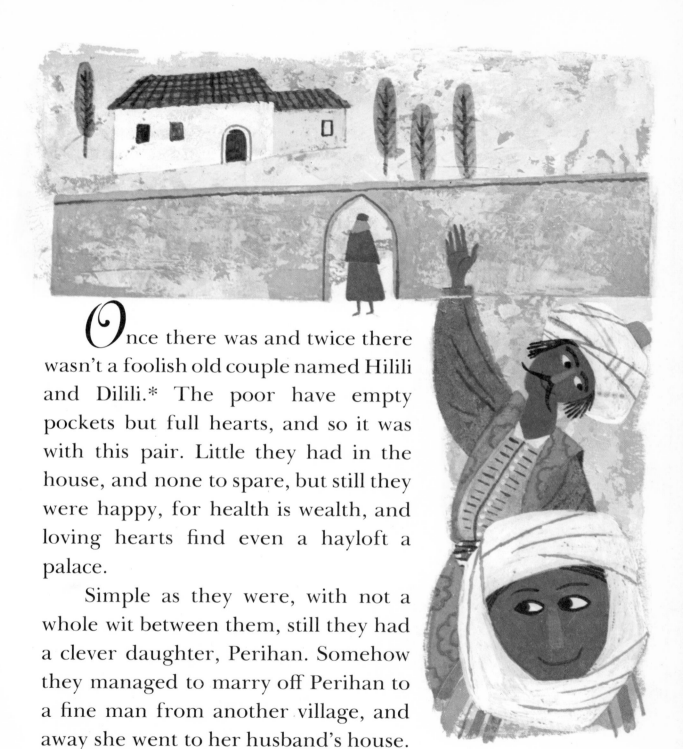

Once there was and twice there wasn't a foolish old couple named Hilili and Dilili.* The poor have empty pockets but full hearts, and so it was with this pair. Little they had in the house, and none to spare, but still they were happy, for health is wealth, and loving hearts find even a hayloft a palace.

Simple as they were, with not a whole wit between them, still they had a clever daughter, Perihan. Somehow they managed to marry off Perihan to a fine man from another village, and away she went to her husband's house.

*The Turks pronounce these names *Huh-luh-luh* and *Duh-luh-luh*.

Perihan's husband was well off, and they had a fine comfortable home. So busy was Perihan, and so full was her life that she seldom wrote and she never visited, and the old folks missed her sorely. What the heart feels, the mouth must speak, and so one day when Hilili was cooking the meat for dinner she said, "Dilili?"

Dilili looked up from the stump of a broom he

was mending. "Yes, Hilili?"

"I miss our daughter. If I could just visit her once, I would be content. Should we go to see her?"

The old man had been thinking along much the same lines as his wife. If Perihan did not come to them, then they must go to her, and go they would.

"To a lonely heart, a greeting is worth a thousand liras," he said. "Let us start today."

The matter was no sooner decided than Hilili made ready to go. She put a heavy lid on the kettle to keep the meat till their return. Then she slipped into her worn shoes and drew her black woolen shawl over her face and shoulders.

As for Dilili, he had the cottage to think of.

"Trust in God, but first tie your camel," he reminded his wife, as he took the rusty door key from its peg on the wall. Stepping into his shoes, he followed his wife across the big black stone that was their doorstep. After carefully locking the door, he lifted up a corner of the stone and slipped the key under it.

Then the two old folks set their faces and their footsteps toward their daughter's village.

Just as they were turning for a last look at their little cottage, they heard the *tukker-tukker* of a horse coming down the dusty road.

"Oh, Dilili!" said the old wife. "Suppose that horseman should take the key from under our black stone, and suppose he should open our door and take the lid off our kettle and eat our meat?"

"It's an open door that invites callers," said Dilili. "All the same, there is nothing to be lost by caution." And as the horseman drew to a walk alongside them, the old man said:

"Oh, horseman! My wife and I are going on a journey. Be sure not to go to our little house and lift up the black stone and take the key, and be sure not to open the door and take the lid off the kettle and eat our meat. We'll be wanting it later, for travel makes a man hungry."

"Indeed it does," the stranger agreed. "And I wish you both well on your journey."

He sat on his horse as the old couple shuffled off out of sight down the road. Then, because travel *does* make a man hungry, of course he rode straight to the old couple's cottage. Of course he took the key from under the black stone and opened the door, and of course he took the lid off the kettle and ate the meat.

He ate and ate, until there was only a small scrap left for the black fly that buzzed in through the open door and settled down to feast in the kettle. Satisfied at last, the horseman put the lid back on. Then he locked the door and slipped the key under the black stone and mounted his horse and rode away, with never so much as a look behind at the little cottage.

13

As for Hilili and Dilili, they walked and walked. But a good companion shortens the longest road, and toward evening of a gray day, they arrived at their daughter's house.

A fine house it was, too, with a tile roof, and glass in all the windows, and buildings at the back for the animals—the horses and cattle and turkeys and roosters and ducks and hens and geese. Yes, it was plain that Perihan's husband was a wealthy man—perhaps almost a padishah—and much too grand for them.

Nevertheless, it was their daughter they had come to see, so they borrowed courage enough to knock on the door. In a moment, there stood Perihan.

"Welcome!" she cried, for grand as her new house was, her heart was still the heart of a good daughter.

14

"We feel welcome," her parents answered, glad of her warm greeting. Leaving their dusty shoes at the doorstep, Hilili and Dilili followed Perihan into a fine room, with couches all about the walls, and rich, soft pillows on the couches.

There was much they had to talk about, but first the old couple must be made clean and comfortable. While the servants went to prepare baths for the travelers, Perihan herself brought them steaming cups of coffee — not the common brew, flat as chestnut water, but good Turkish coffee with proper crests of foam. Hilili and Dilili were happy indeed that they had come.

16

Now Perihan, though she loved her parents dearly, was in truth anxious about their visit, for her husband did not know that her parents had between them only wit enough to salt one dolma.

But luckily, as they sat at dinner with their fine son-in-law, Hilili and Dilili said little or nothing. One is wise, after all, to keep a short hand at table and a short tongue in company, they had agreed. And they gave themselves over to the pleasures of a fine meal, with yoghurt soup and shish kebab and snowy rice pilav and foaming cups of coffee.

17

The evening passed quickly enough, and the time drew near for the old folks to go to bed. Now matters had gone better than she expected, but Perihan had no wish to tempt fortune any further. She decided to have her parents sleep as far away from her husband as she could manage. Calling her servants, Perihan sent them to make up a bed for the guests in the attic, and not long afterwards the old couple tucked in for the night.

The stars climbed the heavens while Hilili and Dilili talked about the blessings that were Perihan's and marveled at the good fortune that had fallen to the daughter of two as simple as they.

While they lay talking, Hilili sniffed suddenly, and then she sniffed again. "Dilili?" said she.

"Yes, Hilili," the old man answered, half asleep on the good down pillow.

"I smell something. Do you suppose it can be the salve our daughter uses on her face to keep her looking so young and beautiful?"

"It may be," said Dilili. "Why don't you try some and see?"

"Let's both try some," said Hilili.

19

So the old couple got up and felt around in the dark until they found what they were looking for. They rubbed their faces and necks and arms with the salve, and then they went to sleep.

As it happened, the salve that they found was tar, and by morning they were both stuck fast to the bed. How could they ever get up and be ready for breakfast?

Perihan waited and waited for her parents to come to the table. Tea was ready and the breakfast was laid out, and still they didn't come down. So up she went to the attic to see what her parents were about, and there they were, caught like birds in a net, and none the wiser.

21

22

"Oh!" said Perihan. "What am I going to do now?"

She called the servants and told them to rub her parents with oil to soften the tar, and to make their baths ready and clean them thoroughly. "But don't say a word about this to my husband," she warned them.

That day went well enough, but as evening came on, Perihan thought long and longer about having her parents in the attic again. She finally decided to have the servants make up the old couple's bed in the poultry house, and that night Hilili and Dilili went to bed with the chickens and geese.

As they lay there talking of this and that, the geese and the hens and the ducks were gurgling and quack-quacking. Finally Hilili said, "Dilili?"

"Yes, Hilili?"

"I think our daughter has been too busy to take good care of her poultry. The poor things are so full of lice they can't sleep! Let's get up and give them a good bath and make them nice and clean, and then they can sleep."

Well, the old folks stirred their bones out of their warm bed to help Perihan. Dilili built a fire and heated a big pot of water, and when it was boiling Hilili took two ducks by the legs and dipped them in for their baths. Sure enough, there was no gurgling or quack-quacking from them any more.

So Hilili and Dilili took all the rest of the poultry in hand, two by two, and dipped them into the boiling water very nicely and quietly, until there wasn't a sound in the poultry house.

In the morning when the servant came
to call the old couple for breakfast, she
found all the poultry dead of their baths.
She hastened to tell Perihan about it. When
Perihan went running out to the poultry
house to see for herself, there were the
old folks, waiting to tell her what they
had done for her.

"Why did you do it? Oh, why did you
do it?" she cried.

Dilili smiled happily. "To help you,
my daughter," he answered. "You were too
busy to take good care of your poultry, and
the poor things were so full of lice they
couldn't sleep."

Poor Perihan! What was she to do? It is easy to say "Come!" and difficult to say "Go!" But one thing was certain: her parents must set their faces for home that very day.

"Surely your little cottage must be needing you," Perihan said gently. "Here, I have some things for you to take home with you." And she gave them each a pair of warm boots and a bolt of bright-colored cloth and a ball of yarn.

So the old folks took leave of Perihan and started back to their own cottage. They went a little; they went far. They went straight over rivers and dales, till at length they came to a place where there was snow. And there in the snow were two black crows.

"Oh, Dilili!" cried Hilili.

"What, Hilili?"

"Look at those crows, poor things—out there in the snow, and on their bare feet! Let's give them our nice warm boots."

He gives twice who gives quickly, so the old folks threw their new boots to the crows and went on their way. As they walked they came to a place where there were some gnarled old olive trees. The wind was blowing, and the branches creaked and rubbed on each other, and the shaking boughs groaned.

"Oh," said Hilili.

"What, Hilili?"

"Don't you see how those trees are shaking? How cold they must be, all bare, without anything to keep them warm. What can we do?"

"Well," said Dilili, "we have the cloth our daughter gave us."

"Oh, Dilili, how clever you are! And we have our yarn, too."

In no time at all they had wrapped some cloth around each tree and tied it snugly with yarn. "There," said Hilili. "Now you'll be nice and warm."

29

The old couple started on their way again. Before long they arrived at their little cottage. They were cold and hungry and very glad to be home.

Dilili took the key from under the black stone on the doorstep and opened the door, and they went in. They went straight to the kettle, and Hilili took off the lid. But there was no good brown meat in the kettle — nothing but a big black fly that buzzed from the bottom and flew around the room.

"Now how do you suppose that fly got in there?" asked Hilili.

Dilili said, "My, he must have been hungry, to eat all our meat!"

Just then the fly settled on Hilili's fore-head. "Hfff!" Hilili blew a good stout breath up over her nose to drive the fly away. But the fly stayed there.

And "Hfffff!" Hilili blew again, harder. But the fly stayed there.

And "Hffffff!" she blew for the third time, even harder. But the fly still stayed there.

This was too much for Dilili. Wanting to help his wife, he picked up the broom from the fireside, and *whack!* he killed the fly!

"There!" he said with satisfaction. "That's the end of *that* fly."

Hilili said nothing at all.